High Waving
Heather

THE BRONTËS

D0587370

A Phoenix Paperback

Selected Poems by the Brontës first published
by J. M. Dent in 1993

This abridged edition published in 1996 by Phoenix
a division of Orion Books Ltd
Orion House, 5 Upper St Martin's Lane, London WC2H 9EA

ISBN 1 85799 545 7

Typeset by Deltatype Ltd, Ellesmere Port, Cheshire
Printed in Great Britain by Clays Ltd, St Ives plc.

Contents

CHARLOTTE BRONTË

Marion's Song

He is gone, and all grandeur has fled from the mountain;
All beauty departed from stream and from fountain;
    A dark veil is hung
      O'er the bright sky of gladness;
      And where birds sweetly sung
    There's a murmur of sadness.
  The wind sings with a warning tone
    Through many a shadowy tree;
I hear, in every passing moan,
    The voice of destiny.

Then, O Lord of the waters! the Great! and All-seeing!
Preserve, in Thy mercy, his safety and being;
    May he trust in Thy might
      When the dark storm is howling,
      And the blackness of night
    Over heaven is scowling.
  But may the sea flow glidingly
    With gentle summer waves;
And silent may all tempests lie
    Chained in Aeolian caves!

Yet, though ere he returnest, long years will have
      vanished,
Sweet hope from my bosom shall never be banished:
    I will think of the time
     When his step, lightly bounding,
      Shall be heard on the rock
     Where the cataract is sounding:
   When the banner of his father's host
    Shall be unfurled on high
  To welcome back the pride and boast
    Of England's chivalry!

Yet tears will flow forth while of hope I am singing;
Still Despair her dark shadow is over me flinging;
     But when he's far away,
    I will pluck the wild flower
     On bank and on brae
     At the still, moonlight hour;
  And I will twine for him a wreath
    Low in the fairies' dell;
  Methought I heard the night-wind breathe
    That solemn word, 'Farewell!'

Lines on Bewick

The cloud of recent death is past away,
   But yet a shadow lingers o'er his tomb

To tell that the pale standard of decay
   Is reared triumphant o'er life's sullied bloom.

But now the eye bedimmed by tears may gaze
   On the fair lines his gifted pencil drew,
The tongue unfaltering speak its meed of praise
   When we behold those scenes to Nature true –

True to the common Nature that we see
   In England's sunny fields, her hills and vales,
On the wild bosom of her storm-dark sea
   Still heaving to the wind that o'er it wails.

How many winged inhabitants of air,
   How many plume-clad floaters of the deep,
The mighty artist drew in forms as fair
   As those that now the skies and waters sweep;

From the great eagle, with his lightning eye,
   His tyrant glance, his talons dyed in blood,
To the sweet breather-forth of melody,
   The gentle merry minstrel of the wood.

Each in his attitude of native grace
   Looks on the grazer life-like, free and bold,
And if the rocks be his abiding place
   Far off appears the winged marauder's hold.

But if the little builder rears his nest
   In the still shadow of green tranquil trees,
And singing sweetly 'mid the silence blest
   Sits a meet emblem of untroubled peace,

'A change comes o'er the spirit of our dream,' –
   Woods wave around in crested majesty;
We almost feel the joyous sunshine's beam
   And hear the breath of the sweet south go by.

Our childhood's days return again in thought,
   We wander in a land of love and light,
And mingled memories, joy – and sorrow – fraught
   Gush on our hearts with overwhelming might.

Sweet flowers seem gleaming 'mid the tangled grass
   Sparkling with spray-drops from the rushing rill,
And as these fleeting visions fade and pass
   Perchance some pensive tears our eyes may fill.

These soon are wiped away, again we turn
   With fresh delight to the enchanted page
Where pictured thoughts that breathe and speak and
      burn
   Still please alike our youth and riper age.

There rises some lone rock all wet with surge
   And dashing billows glimmering in the light

Of a wan moon, whose silent rays emerge
   From clouds that veil their lustre, cold and bright.

And there 'mongst reeds upon a river's side
   A wild bird sits, and brooding o'er her nest
Still guards the priceless gems, her joy and pride,
   Now ripening 'neath her hope-enlivened breast.

We turn the page: before the expectant eye
   A traveller stands lone on some desert heath;
The glorious sun is passing from the sky
   While fall his farewell rays on all beneath;

O'er the far hills a purple veil seems flung,
   Dim herald of the coming shades of night;
E'en now Diana's lamp aloft is hung,
   Drinking full radiance from the fount of light.

Oh, when the solemn wind of midnight sighs,
   Where will the lonely traveller lay his head?
Beneath the tester of the star-bright skies
   On the wild moor he'll find a dreary bed.

Now we behold a marble Naiad placed
   Beside a fountain on her sculptured throne
Her bending form with simplest beauty graced,
   Her white robes gathered in a snowy zone.

She from a polished vase pours forth a stream
    Of sparkling water to the waves below
Which roll in light and music, while the gleam
    Of sunshine flings through shade a golden glow.

A hundred fairer scenes these leaves reveal;
    But there are tongues that injure while they praise;
I cannot speak the rapture that I feel
    When on the work of such a mind I gaze.

Then farewell, Bewick, genius' favoured son,
    Death's sleep is on the thee, all thy woes are past;
From earth departed, life and labour done,
    Eternal peace and rest are thine at last.

Retrospection

We wove a web in childhood,
    A web of sunny air;
We dug a spring in infancy
    Of water pure and fair;

We sowed in youth a mustard seed,
    We cut an almond rod;
We are now grown up to riper age:
    Are they withered in the sod?

Are they blighted, failed and faded,
    Are they mouldered back to clay?
For life is darkly shaded,
    And its joys fleet fast away!

Stanzas

If thou be in a lonely place,
    If one hour's calm be thine,
As Evening bends her placid face
    O'er this sweet day's decline;
If all the earth and all the heaven
    Now look serene to thee,
As o'er them shuts the summer even,
    One moment – think of me!

Pause, in the lane, returning home;
    'Tis dusk, it will be still:
Pause near the elm, a sacred gloom
    Its breezeless boughs will fill.
Look at that soft and golden light,
    High in the unclouded sky;
Watch the last bird's belated flight,
    As it flits silent by.

Hark! for a sound upon the wind,
    A step, a voice, a sigh;

If all be still, then yield thy mind,
   Unchecked, to memory.
If thy love were like mine, how blest
   That twilight hour would seem,
When, back from the regretted Past,
   Returned our early dream!

If thy love were like mine, how wild
   Thy longings, even to pain,
For sunset soft, and moonlight mild,
   To bring that hour again?
But oft, when in thine arms I lay,
   I've seen thy dark eyes shine,
And deeply felt their changeful ray
   Spoke other love than mine.

My love is almost anguish now,
   It beats so strong and true;
'Twere rapture, could I deem that thou
   Such anguish ever knew.
I have been but thy transient flower,
   Thou wert my god divine,
Till checked by death's congealing power,
   This heart must throb for thine.

And well my dying hour were blest,
   If life's expiring breath
Should pass, as thy lips gently prest

My forehead cold in death;
And sound my sleep would be, and sweet,
   Beneath the churchyard tree,
If sometimes in thy heart should beat
   One pulse, still true to me.

Passion

Some have won a wild delight,
   By daring wilder sorrow;
Could I gain thy love to-night,
   I'd hazard death to-morrow.

Could the battle-struggle earn
   One kind glance from thine eye,
How this withering heart would burn,
   The heady fight to try!

Welcome nights of broken sleep,
   And days of carnage cold,
Could I deem that thou wouldst weep
   To hear my perils told.

Tell me, if with wandering bands
   I roam full far away,
Wilt thou to those distant lands
   In spirit ever stray!

Wild, long, a trumpet sounds afar;
    Bid me – bid me go
Where Seik and Briton meet in war,
    On Indian Sutlej's flow.

Blood has dyed the Sutlej's waves
    With scarlet stain, I know;
Indus' borders yawn with graves,
    Yet, command me go!

Though rank and high the holocaust
    Of nations steams to heaven,
Glad I'd join the death-doomed host,
    Were but the mandate given.

Passion's strength should nerve my arm,
    Its ardour stir my life,
Till human force to that dread charm
Should yield and sink in wild alarm,
    Like trees to tempest-strife.

If, hot from war, I seek thy love,
    Darest thou turn aside?
Darest thou then my fire reprove,
    By scorn, and maddening pride?

No – my will shall yet control
    Thy will so high and free,

And love shall tame that haughty soul –
    Yes – tenderest love for me.

I'll read my triumph in thine eyes,
    Behold, and prove the change;
Then leave, perchance, my noble prize,
    Once more in arms to range.

I'd die when all the foam is up,
    The bright wine sparkling high;
Nor wait till in the exhausted cup
    Life's dull dregs only lie.

Then Love thus crowned with sweet reward,
    Hope blessed with fulness large,
I'd mount the saddle, draw the sword,
    And perish in the charge!

Evening Solace

The human heart has hidden treasures,
    In secret kept, in silence sealed; –
The thoughts, the hopes, the dreams, the pleasures,
    Whose charms were broken if revealed.
And days may pass in gay confusion,
    And nights in rosy riot fly,
While, lost in Fame's or Wealth's illusion,
    The memory of the Past may die.

But there are hours of lonely musing,
Such as in evening silence come,
When, soft as birds their pinions closing,
    The heart's best feelings gather home.
Then in our souls there seems to languish
    A tender grief that is not woe;
And thoughts that once wrung groans of anguish,
    Now cause but some mild tears to flow.

And feelings, once as strong as passions,
    Float softly back – a faded dream;
Our own sharp griefs and wild sensations,
    The tale of others' sufferings seem.
Oh! when the heart is freshly bleeding,
    How longs it for that time to be,
When, through the mist of years receding,
    Its woes live but in reverie!

And it can dwell on moonlight glimmer,
    On evening shade and loneliness;
And, while the sky grows dim and dimmer,
    Feel no untold and strange distress –
Only a deeper impulse given
    By lonely hour and darkened room,
To solemn thoughts that soar to heaven
    Seeking a life and world to come.

On the Death of Anne Brontë

There's little joy in life for me,
  And little terror in the grave;
I've lived the parting hour to see
  Of one I would have died to save.

Calmly to watch the failing breath,
  Wishing each sigh might be the last;
Longing to see the shade of death
  O'er those beloved features cast.

The cloud, the stillness that must part
  The darling of my life from me;
And then to thank God from my heart,
  To thank Him well and fervently;

Although I knew that we had lost
  The hope and glory of our life;
And now, benighted, tempest-tossed,
  Must bear alone the weary strife.

PATRICK BRANWELL BRONTË

Augusta

Augusta! Though I'm far away
   Across the dark blue sea
Still eve and morn and night and day
   Will I remember Thee!

And though I cannot see thee nigh
   Or hear thee speak to me
Thy look and voice and memory
   Shall not forgotten be

I stand upon this Island shore
   A single hour alone
And see the Atlantic swell before
   With sullen surging tone

While high in heaven the full Moon glides
   Above the breezy deep
Unmoved by waves or winds or tides
   That far beneath her sweep

She marches through this midnight air
   So silent and divine
With not a wreath of vapour there
   To dim her silver shine

For every cloud through ether driven
   Has settled far below
And round the unmeasured skirts of heaven
   Their whitened fleeces glow

They join and part and pass away
   Beyond the heaving sea
So mutable and restless they
   So still and changeless she

Those clouds have melted into air
   Those waves have sunk to sleep
But clouds renewed are rising there
   And fresh waves crowd the deep

How like the chaos of my soul
   Where visions ever rise
And thoughts and passions ceaseless roll
   And tumult never dies

Each fancy but the former's grave
   And germ of that to come

While all are fleeting as the wave
    That chafes itself to foam

I said that full Moon glides on high
    Howe'er the world repines
And in its own untroubled sky
    For ever smiles and shines

So dark'ning o'er my anxious brow
    Though thicken cares and pain
Within my Heart Augusta thou
    For ever shalt remain

And Thou art not that wintry moon
    With its melancholy ray
But where thou shinest is summer noon
    And bright and perfect day

The Moon sinks down as sinks the night
    But Thou beam'st brightly on
She only shines with borrowed light
    But Thine is all Thine Own!

The Doubter's Hymn

Life is a passing sleep
    Its deeds a troubled dream

And death the dread awakening
　　To daylight's dawning beam

　　We sleep without a thought
　　Of what is past and o'er
Without a glimpse of consciousness
　　Of aught that lies before

　　We dream and on our sight
　　A thousand visions rise
Some dark as Hell some heavenly bright
　　But all are phantasies

　　We wake and oh how fast
　　These mortal visions fly!
Forgot amid the wonders vast
　　Of immortality!

　　And oh! when we arise
　　With 'wildered gaze to see
The aspect of those morning skies
　　Where will that waking be?

　　How will that Future seem?
　　What is Eternity?
Is Death the sleep? – Is Heaven the Dream?
　　Life the reality?

Mary's Prayer

Remember me when Death's dark wing
   Has borne me far from thee;
When, freed from all this suffering,
   My grave shall cover me.

Remember me, and, if I die
   To perish utterly,
Yet shrined within thy memory
   Thy Heart my Heaven shall be!

'Twas all I wished, when first I gave
   This hand unstained and free,
That I from thence might ever have
   A place, my lord, with thee.

So, if from off my dying bed
   Thou'dst banish misery,
Oh say that when I'm cold and dead
   Though wilt remember me!

'The desolate earth'

The desolate earth, the wintry sky,
The ceaseless rain-showers driving by –
   The farewell of the year –

Though drear the sight, and sad the sound,
While bitter winds are wailing round,
Nor hopes depress, nor thoughts confound,
  Nor waken sigh or tear.

For, as it moans, December's wind
Brings many varied thoughts to mind
  Upon its storm-drenched wing,
Of words, not said 'mid sunshine gay,
Of deeds, not done in summer's day,
Yet which, when joy has passed away,
  Will strength to sorrow bring.

For, when the leaves are glittering bright,
And green hills lie in noonday night,
  The present only lives;
But, when within my chimnies roar
The chidings of the stormy shower,
The feeble present loses power,
  The mighty past survives.

I cannot think – as roses blow,
And streams sound gently in their flow,
  And clouds shine bright above –
Of aught but childhood's happiness,
Of joys unshadowed by distress
Or voices tuned the ear to bless
  Or faces made to love.

But, when these winter evenings fall
Like dying nature's funeral pall,
  The Soul gains strength to say
That – not aghast at stormy skies –
That – not bowed down by miseries, –
Its thoughts have will and power to rise
  Above the present day.

So, winds amid yon leafless ash,
And yon swollen streamlet's angry dash,
  And yon wet howling sky,
Recall the victories of mind
O'er bitter heavens and stormy wind
And all the wars of humankind –
  Man's mightiest victory!

The darkness of a dungeon's gloom,
So oft ere death the spirit's tomb,
  Could not becloud those eyes
Which first revealed to mortal sight
A thousand unknown worlds of light,
And that *one* grave shines best by night
  Where Galileo lies.

But – into drearier dungeons thrown,
With bodies bound, whose minds were gone –
  Tasso's immortal strain,
Despite the tyrant's stern decree,

Mezentius-like – rose fresh and free
And sang of Salem's liberty
  Forgetful of his chain;

And thou, great rival of his song,
Whose seraph-wings so swift and strong
  Left this world far behind,
Though poor, neglected, blind and old,
The clouds round Paradise unrolled
And in immortal accents told
  Misery must bow to mind.

See, in a garret bare and low,
While mighty London roars below,
  One poor man seated lone;
No favourite child of fortune he,
But owned as hers by Poverty,
His rugged brow, his stooping knee,
  Speak woe and want alone.

Now, who would guess that yonder form,
Scarce worth being beaten by life's storm,
  Could e'er be known to fame?
Yet England's love and England's tongue,
And England's heart, shall reverence long
The wisdom deep, the courage strong,
  Of English *Johnson's* name.

Like him – foredoomed through life to bear
The anguish of the heart's despair
   That pierces spirit through –
Sweet Cowper, 'mid his weary years,
Led through a rayless vale of tears,
Poured gentle wisdom on our ears,
   And his was English too.

But Scotland's desolate hills can show
How mind can triumph over woe,
   For many a cottage there,
Where ceaseless toil from day to day
Scarce keeps grim want one hour away,
Could show if known how great the sway
   Of spirit o'er despair.

And he whose natural music fills
Each wind that sweeps her heathy hills,
   Bore up with manliest brow
'Gainst griefs that ever filled his breast,
'Gainst toils that never gave him rest,
So, though grim fate Burns' life oppressed,
   His soul it could not bow.

Lord Nelson

Man thinks too often that the ills of Life,
Its fruitless labours and its causeless strife,

Its fell disease, grim want and cankering care,
Must wage 'gainst Spirit a successful war;
That faint and feeble proves the struggling soul
'Mid the dark waves that ever round it roll;
That it can never triumph or feel free
While pain its body holds or poverty.

   No words of mine have power to rouse the brain
Distressed with grief – the body bowed with pain;
They will not hear me if I prove how high
Man's soul can soar o'er body's misery.

But, where orations long and deep and loud
Are weak as air to move the listening crowd,
A single word, just then, if timely spoken,
The mass inert has roused, their silence broken,
And driven them shouting for revenge or fame,
Trampling on fear or death, led by a *single Name*.
So now to him whose worn out soul decays
'Neath nights of sleepless pain or toilsome days
Who thinks his feeble frame must vainly long
To tread the footsteps of the bold and strong,
Who thinks that, born beneath a lowly star,
He cannot climb those heights he sees from far,
To him I name one name (it needs but one)
NELSON, a world's defence, a kingdom's noblest son.

   Ah! little child, torn early from thy home,
Over a desolate waste of waves to roam,

I see thy fair hair streaming in the wind
Wafted from green hills left so far behind –
A farewell given to thy English home,
And hot tears dimming all thy views of fame to come!

Then thou perhaps wert clinging to the mast,
Rocked high above the Northern Ocean's waste,
Stern accents only shouted from beneath,
Above, the keen wind's bitter biting breath,
And thy young eyes attentive to descry
The Ice-blink gleaming 'neath a Greenland sky;
All round, the presages of strife and storm
Engirdling thy young heart and feeble form;
Each change thy frame endured were fit to be
The total round of common destiny.
For next, upon the wild Mosquito shore
San Juan's guns their deadly thunders pour,
Though deadlier far that pestilential sky
Whose hot winds only whispered who should die.
Yet, while – forgotten – all their honours won –
Strong frames lay rotting 'neath a tropic sun
And mighty breasts heaved in death's agony,
Left him to dare his darts through many a year
Of storm-tossed life – unbowed by pain or fear.

Death saw him laid on rocky Teneriffe,
Where sailors bore away their bleeding chief,
Struck down by shot and beaten back by fate,
Yet keeping Iron front and soul elate.

Death saw him, calm, off Copenhagen's shore,
Amid a thousand guns' death-dealing roar,
Triumphant riding o'er a fallen foe,
With hand prepared to strike, and heart to spare the
      blow.

Death touched, but left him, when a tide of blood
Stained the dark waves of Egypt's ancient flood,
When mighty L'Orient fired the midnight sky
And clouds dimmed Napoleon's destiny,
When 'neath that blaze flashed redly sea and shore,
When far Aboukir shook beneath its roar,
Then fell on all one mighty pause of dread
As if wide heaven were shattered overhead.
But from his pallet where the hero lay
His forehead laced with blood and pale as clay
He rose, revived by that tremendous call,
Forgot the blow which lately made him fall
And bade the affrighted battle hurry on,
Nor thought of pain or rest till victory was won.

I see him set – his coffin by his chair –
With pain-worn cheeks and wind-dishevelled hair,
A little shattered wreck from many a day
Of ocean storm and battle passed away,
Prepared at any hour God bade to die
But not to stop or rest or strike or fly;
While like a burning reed his spirit's flame

Brightened as it consumed its mortal frame.
He heard death tapping at his cabin door,
He knew his light'ning course must soon be o'er.
That he must meet the grim yet welcome guest,
Not on a palace bed of downy rest
But where the stormy waters rolled below,
And pealed, above, the thunders of the foe;
That no calm sleep must smooth a slow decay
Till scarce the watchers knew life passed away;
But stifling agony and gushing gore
Must tell the moments of his parting hour.
He knew, but smiled, for – as that Polar Star
For thousand years as then had shone from far
While all had changed beneath its changeless sky –
So what to earth belongs, on earth must die.
While he, all soul, should only take his flight
Like yon, through time, a soft and steady light;
Like yon, to England's sailors given to be
The guardian of their fleets, the pole star of the free.

A vessel lies in England's proudest port,
Where venerating thousands oft resort,
And though ships round her anchor, bold and gay,
They seek her only in her grim decay;
They tread her decks, all tenantless, with eyes
Of musing awe, not vulgar vain surprise;
They enter in a cabin, dark and low,
And o'er its time-stained floor in reverence bow.

There's nought to see but rafters worn and old.
No mirrored walls, no cornice bright with gold;
Yon packet, steaming through the smoky haze
Seems fitter far to suit the wanderers' gaze.
But – 'tis not present times they look on now,
They gaze on six and thirty years ago;
They see where fell the 'Thunder-bolt of war'
On the storm-swollen waves of *Trafalgar*;
They see the spot where fell a star of glory,
The Finis to one pace of England's story;
They read a tale to wake their pain and pride
In that brass plate engraved – 'HERE NELSON DIED.'

As 'wise Cornelius' from his mirror bade
A veil of formless cloudiness to fade,
Till gleamed before the awe-struck gazer's eye
Scenes still to come or passed for ever by,
So let me, standing in this darksome room,
Roll back its shapelessness of mourning gloom
And show the morn and evening of a Sun
The memory of whose light still cheers old England on.

Where ceaseless showers obscure the misty vale,
And winter winds through leafless osiers wail,
Beside yon swollen torrent rushing wild
Sits calm, amid the storm, that fair-haired child.
He *cannot* cross – so full the waters flow –
So bold his little heart – he *will not* go.

He has been absent, wandering many an hour,
As wild waves toss a solitary flower,
While from the old Rectory, his distant home,
'All hands' to seek their missing darling roam;
And *one* – his mother – with instinctive love,
Like that which guides aright the timid dove,
Finds her dear child, his cheeks all rain-bedewed,
The unconscious victim of those tempests rude,
And, panting, asks him why he tarries there –
Did he not dread his fate, his danger fear?
That child replies – all smiling 'mid the storm –
'Say Mother – what is this "fear"? I never saw his form.'

Oft since, he saw the waters howling round,
Oft heard unmoved, as then, the tempest sound,
Oft stood unshaken, death and danger near,
But knew no more than then the phantom *Fear*.

Now wave the wand again – let England's shore
Be lost amid a distant ocean's roar;
Return again this cabin, dark and grim,
Beheld through smoke-wreaths, indistinct and dim.
'Where is my child?' methinks the mother cries:
No – far away that mother's grave stone lies!
Where is her child? He is not surely here
Where reign 'mid storm and darkness Death and FEAR.

A prostrate form lies 'neath a double shade
By stifling smoke and blackened rafters made,
With head that backward rolls whene'er it tries
From its hard thunder-shaken bed to rise.
Methought I saw a brightness on its breast,
As if in royal orders decked and dressed;
But that wan face, those grey locks crimson-dyed,
Have nought to do with human power or pride,
Where Death his mandate writes on that white brow:
'Thy earthly course is done – come with me now!'
Stern faces o'er this figure, weeping bend
As they had lost a father and a friend,
And all unnoticed burst yon conquering cheer
Since HE their glorious chief is dying here.
They heed it not; but, with rekindling eye,
As he even Death would conquer ere he die,
Asks: 'What was't? What deed had England done?
What ships had struck, was victory nobly won?
Did Collingwood – did Trowbridge face the foe?
Whose ship was first in fight, who dealt the sternest
        blow?'

I could not hear the answer, lost and drowned
In that tremendous crash of earthquake sound,
But I could see the dying hero smile,
For pain and sickness vanquished humbly bowed the
        while
TO SOUL, that soared prophetic o'er their sway,

And saw beyond Death's night Fame's glorious day,
That deemed no bed so easy as the tomb
In old Westminster's hero-sheltering gloom;
That knew the laurel round his dying brow
Must bloom for ever as it flourished now,
That felt this pain he paid was cheaply given
For endless fame on earth and joy in heaven.
It was a smile as sweet as ever shone
On that wan face in childhood long since gone,
A smile that asked as plainly:- 'What is fear?'
As then unnoticed though as then so near!
That spirit cared not that his wornout form
Was soon to be a comrade of the worm,
Nor shuddered at the icy hand of Death,
So soon – so painfully to stop his breath.

The guns were thundering fainter on his ear;
More, fading fast from sight that cabin drear;
The place, the hour became less clearly known:
He only felt that his great work was done,
That one brave heart was kneeling at his side,
So, murmuring 'Kiss me, Hardy,' Nelson, smiling, died.

But when *I* think upon that awful day
When all I know or love must fade away,
When, after weeks perhaps of agony,
Without a hope of aught to succour me,

I must lie back and close my eyes upon
The parting glories of God's holy sun
And feel his warmth I never more must know
Mocking my wretched frame of pain and woe,
Yes – feel his light is brightening up the sky
As shining clouds and summer airs pass by,
While I a shrouded corpse this bed must leave
To lie forgotten in my dreary grave,
The world all smiles above my covering clay,
I silent – senseless – festering fast away.

And if my children 'mongst the churchyard stones,
Years hence, should see a few brown mouldering bones,
Perhaps a skull that seems with hideous grin
To mock at all this world takes pleasure in,
They'd only from the unsightly relics turn,
Or into ranker grass the fragments spurn,
Nor know that those were the remains of him
Whom they remember like a happy dream;
Who kissed and danced them on a father's knee
In long departed hours of happy Infancy!

O Mighty Being! give me strength to dare
The certain fate – the dreadful hour to bear –
As thou didst, Nelson, 'mid that awful roar,
Lying pale with mortal sickness – choked with gore,
Yet thinking of thine ENGLAND, saved that hour
From her great Foeman's empire-crushing power;
Of thy poor frame, so gladly given to free

Her thousand happy homes from slavery;
Of stainless name for her – of endless fame for Thee!

Give me, Great God, give all beneath Thy sway,
Soul to command and body to obey;
When dangers threat – a heart to beat more high;
When doubts confuse – a more observant eye;
When fate would crush us down – a steadier arm;
A firmer front – as stronger beats the storm.
We are Thy likeness – give us on to go
Through life's long march of chance and change to woe,
Resolved Thine image shall be sanctified
By humble confidence, not foolish pride.
We have our task set – let us do it well;
Nor barter ease on earth with pain in hell.
We have our talents from Thy Treasury given:
Let us return Thee good account in Heaven.

I see Thy world – this age – is marching on,
Each year more wondrous than its parent gone;
And shall my own drag heavily and slow,
With wish to rise, yet grovelling far below?
Forbid it, God, who madst (me) what I am,
Nor made to honour let me bow to shame;
But as yon moon that *seems* through clouds to glide
Whose dark breasts ever strive her beams to hide
Shines *really* heedless of their earthly sway
In her own heaven of glory far away,

So may my soul, that seems involved below,
In life's conflicting mists of care and woe,
Far, far remote – from its own heaven – look down
On clouds of shining fleece or stormy frown,
And while – so oft eclipsed – men pity me,
Gaze steadfast at their life's inconstancy,
And feel myself, like her, at home in heaven with Thee.

On Peaceful Death and Painful Life

Why dost thou sorrow for the happy dead?
  For, if their life be lost, their toils are o'er,
  And woe and want can trouble them no more;
Nor ever slept they in an earthly bed
So sound as now they sleep, while dreamless laid
  In the dark chambers of the unknown shore,
  Where Night and Silence guard each sealed door.
So, turn from such as these thy drooping head,
  And mourn the *Dead Alive* – whose spirit flies –
Whose life departs, before his death has come;
  Who knows no Heaven beneath Life's gloomy skies,
Who sees no Hope to brighten up that gloom, –
  'Tis *He* who feels the worm that never dies, –
The *real* death and darkness of the tomb.

EMILY JANE BRONTË

'High waving heather'

High waving heather, 'neath stormy blasts bending,
Midnight and moonlight and bright shining stars;
Darkness and glory rejoicingly blending,
Earth rising to heaven and heaven descending,
Man's spirit away from its drear dongeon sending,
Bursting the fetters and breaking the bars.

All down the mountain-sides, wild forests lending
One mighty voice to the life-giving wind;
Rivers their banks in the jubilee rending,
Fast through the valleys a reckless course wending,
Wilder and deeper their waters extending,
Leaving a desolate desert behind.

Shining and lowering and swelling and dying,
Changing for ever from midnight to noon;
Roaring like thunder, like soft music sighing,
Shadows on shadows advancing and flying,
Lightning-bright flashes the deep gloom defying,
Coming as swiftly and fading as soon.

'The night is darkening round me'

The night is darkening round me,
The wild winds coldly blow;
But a tyrant spell has bound me
And I cannot, cannot go.

The giant trees are bending
Their bare boughs weighed with snow,
The storm is fast descending
And yet I cannot go.

Clouds beyond clouds above me,
Wastes beyond wastes below;
But nothing drear can move me;
I will not, cannot go.

"I'll come when thou art saddest'

I'll come when thou art saddest,
Laid alone in the darkened room;
When the mad day's mirth has vanished,
And the smile of joy is banished
From evening's chilly gloom.

I'll come when the heart's real feeling
Has entire, unbiassed sway,

And my influence o'er thee stealing,
Grief deepening, joy congealing,
Shall bear thy soul away.

Listen, 'tis just the hour,
The awful time for thee;
Dost thou not feel upon thy soul
A flood of strange sensations roll,
Forerunners of a sterner power,
Heralds of me?

Stanzas

A little while, a little while,
The noisy crowd are barred away;
And I can sing and I can smile
A little while I've holyday!

Where wilt thou go, my harassed heart?
Full many a land invites thee now;
And places near and far apart
Have rest for thee, my weary brow.

There is a spot mid barren hills
Where winter howls and driving rain,
But if the dreary tempest chills
There is a light that warms again.

The house is old, the trees are bare
And moonless bends the misty dome
But what on earth is half so dear,
So longed for as the hearth of home?

The mute bird sitting on the stone,
The dank moss dripping from the wall,
The garden-walk with weeds o'er-grown,
I love them – how I love them all!

Shall I go there? or shall I seek
Another clime, another sky,
Where tongues familiar music speak
In accents dear to memory?

Yes, as I mused, the naked room,
The flickering firelight died away
And from the midst of cheerless gloom
I passed to bright, unclouded day –

A little and a lone green lane,
That opened on a common wide;
A distant, dreamy, dim blue chain
Of mountains circling every side;

A heaven so clear, an earth so calm,
So sweet, so soft, so hushed an air
And, deepening still the dream-like charm,
Wild moor-sheep feeding everywhere –

That was the scene; I knew it well,
I knew the path-ways far and near
That winding o'er each billowy swell
Marked out the tracks of wandering deer.

Could I have lingered but an hour
It well had paid a week of toil,
But truth has banished fancy's power;
I hear my dungeon bars recoil –

Even as I stood with raptured eye
Absorbed in bliss so deep and dear
My hour of rest had fleeted by
And given me back to weary care.

Sympathy

There should be no despair for you
While nightly stars are burning,
While evening pours its silent dew
And sunshine gilds the morning.

There should be no despair, though tears
May flow down like a river:
Are not the best beloved of years
Around your heart forever?

They weep – you weep – it must be so;
Winds sigh as you are sighing;
And Winter sheds its grief in snow
Where Autumn's leaves are lying:

Yet these revive, and from their fate
Your fate cannot be parted,
Then journey on, if not elate,
Still, *never* broken-hearted!

The Old Stoic

Riches I hold in light esteem
And Love I laugh to scorn
And lust of Fame was but a dream,
That vanished with the morn –

And if I pray, the only prayer
That moves my lips for me
Is – 'Leave the heart that now I bear
And give me liberty.'

Yes, as my swift days near their goal
'Tis all that I implore –
In life and death a chainless soul,
With courage to endure!

'I see around me tombstones grey'

I see around me tombstones grey
Stretching their shadows far away.
Beneath the turf my footsteps tread
Lie low and lone the silent dead;
Beneath the turf, beneath the mould –
Forever dark, forever cold,
And my eyes cannot hold the tears
That memory hoards from vanished years;
For Time and Death and Mortal pain
Give wounds that will not heal again.
Let me remember half the woe
I've seen and heard and felt below,
And Heaven itself, so pure and blest,
Could never give my spirit rest.
Sweet land of light! thy children fair
Know nought akin to our despair;
Nor have they felt, nor can they tell
What tenants haunt each mortal cell,
What gloomy guests we hold within –
Torments and madness, tears and sin!
Well, may they live in ecstasy
Their long eternity of joy;
At least we would not bring them down
With us to weep, with us to groan.
No – Earth would wish no other sphere
To taste her cup of sufferings drear;

She turns from Heaven a careless eye,
And only mourns that *we* must die!
Ah, mother, what shall comfort thee
In all this boundless misery?
To cheer our eager eyes a while
We see thee smile; how fondly smile!
But who reads not through that tender glow
Thy deep, unutterable woe?
Indeed, no dazzling land above
Can cheat thee of thy children's love.
We all, in life's departing shine,
Our last dear longings blend with thine,
And struggle still and strive to trace
With clouded gaze, thy darling face.
We would not leave our native home
For *any* world beyond the Tomb.
No – rather on thy kindly breast
Let us be laid in lasting rest;
Or waken but to share with thee
A mutual immortality.

Song

The linnet in the rocky dells,
The moor-lark in the air,
The bee among the heather-bells
That hide my lady fair:

The wild deer browse above her breast;
The wild birds raise their brood;
And they, her smiles of love caressed,
Have left her solitude!

I ween, that when the grave's dark wall
Did first her form retain,
They thought their hearts could ne'er recall
The light of joy again.

They thought the tide of grief would flow
Unchecked through future years,
But where is all their anguish now,
And where are all their tears?

Well, let them fight for Honour's breath,
Or Pleasure's shade pursue –
The Dweller in the land of Death
Is changed and careless too.

And if their eyes should watch and weep
Till sorrow's source were dry,
She would not, in her tranquil sleep,
Return a single sigh.

Blow, west wind, by the lonely mound,
And murmur, summer streams,
There is no need of other sound
To soothe my Lady's dreams.

To Imagination

When weary wth the long day's care,
And earthly change from pain to pain,
And lost, and ready to despair,
Thy kind voice calls me back again –
O my true friend, I am not lone
While thou canst speak with such a tone!

So hopeless is the world without,
The world within I doubly prize;
Thy world where guile and hate and doubt
And cold suspicion never rise;
Where thou and I and Liberty
Have undisputed sovereignty.

What matters it, that all around
Danger, and guilt, and darkness lie,
If but within our bosom's bound
We hold a bright, untroubled sky,
Warm with ten thousand mingled rays
Of suns that know no winter days?

Reason indeed may oft complain
For Nature's sad reality,
And tell the suffering heart how vain
Its cherished dreams must always be;
And Truth may rudely trample down
The flowers of Fancy newly blown.

But thou art ever there to bring
The hovering vision back, and breathe
New glories o'er the blighted spring
And call a lovelier life from death,
And whisper with a voice divine
Of real worlds as bright as thine.

I trust not to thy phantom bliss,
Yet still in evening's quiet hour
With never-failing thankfulness
I welcome thee, benignant power,
Sure solacer of human cares
And sweeter hope, when hope despairs.

Plead for Me

Oh, thy bright eyes must answer now,
When Reason, with a scornful brow,
Is mocking at my overthrow;
O thy sweet tongue must plead for me
And tell why I have chosen thee!

Stern Reason is to judgment come
Arrayed in all her forms of gloom:
Wilt though my advocate be dumb?
No, radiant angel, speak and say
Why I did cast the world away;

Why I have persevered to shun
The common paths that others run;
And on a strange road journeyed on
Heedless alike of Wealth and Power –
Of Glory's wreath and Pleasure's flower.

These once indeed seemed Beings divine,
And they perchance heard vows of mine
And saw my offerings on their shrine –
But, careless gifts are seldom prized,
And *mine* were worthily despised.

So with a ready heart I swore
To seek their altar-stone no more;
And gave my spirit to adore
Thee, ever present, phantom thing –
My slave, my comrade, and my King!

A slave because I rule thee still;
Incline thee to my changeful will
And make thy influence good or ill –
A comrade, for by day and night
Thou art my intimate delight –

My Darling Pain that wounds and sears
And wrings a blessing out from tears
By deadening me to earthly cares;
And yet, a king – though prudence well
Have taught thy subject to rebel.

And am I wrong to worship where
Faith cannot doubt nor Hope despair
Since my own soul can grant my prayer?
Speak, God of Visions, plead for me
And tell why I have chosen thee!

Remembrance

Cold in the earth – and the deep snow piled above thee!
Far, far removed, cold in the dreary grave!
Have I forgot, my Only Love, to love thee,
Severed at last by Time's all-severing wave?

Now, when alone, do my thoughts no longer hover
Over the mountains, on that northern shore,
Resting their wings where heath and fern-leaves cover
Thy noble heart for ever, ever more?

Cold in the earth, and fifteen wild Decembers
From those brown hills, have melted into spring –
Faithful indeed is the spirit that remembers
After such years of change and suffering!

Sweet Love of youth, forgive, if I forget thee,
While the World's tide is bearing me along:
Other desires and other hopes beset me,
Hopes which obscure but cannot do thee wrong.

No later light has lightened up my heaven,
No second morn has ever shone for me;
All my life's bliss from thy dear life was given –
All my life's bliss is in the grave with thee.

But when the days of golden dreams had perished
And even Despair was powerless to destroy,
Then did I learn how existence could be cherished
Strengthened and fed without the aid of joy;

Then did I check the tears of useless passion,
Weaned my young soul from yearning after thine;
Sternly denied its burning wish to hasten
Down to that tomb already more than mine!

And even yet, I dare not let it languish,
Dare not indulge in Memory's rapturous pain;
Once drinking deep of that divinest anguish,
How could I seek the empty world again?

Stanzas

Often rebuked, yet always back returning
　　To those first feelings that were born with me,
And leaving busy chase of wealth and learning
　　For idle dreams of things which cannot be:

To-day, I will seek not the shadowy region:
  Its unsustaining vastness waxes drear;
And visions rising, legion after legion,
  Bring the unreal world too strangely near.

I'll walk, but not in old heroic traces,
  And not in paths of high morality,
And not among the half-distinguished faces,
  The clouded forms of long-past history.

I'll walk where my own nature would be leading:
  It vexes me to choose another guide:
Where the gray flocks in ferny glens are feeding;
  Where the wild wind blows on the mountain side.

What have those lonely mountains worth revealing?
  More glory and more grief than I can tell:
The earth that wakes *one* human heart to feeling
  Can centre both the worlds of Heaven and Hell.

The Bluebell

A fine and subtle spirit dwells
    In every little flower,
Each one its own sweet feeling breathes
    With more or less of power.

There is a silent eloquence
    In every wild bluebell,
That fills my softened heart with bliss
    That words could never tell.

Yet I recall, not long ago,
    A bright and sunny day:
'Twas when I led a toilsome life
    So many leagues away.

That day along a sunny road
    All carelessly I strayed
Between two banks where smiling flowers
    Their varied hues displayed.

Before me rose a lofty hill,
    Behind me lay the sea;
My heart was not so heavy then
    As it was wont to be.

Less harassed than at other times
    I saw the scene was fair,
And spoke and laughed to those around,
    As if I knew no care.

But as I looked upon the bank,
    My wandering glances fell
Upon a little trembling flower,
    A single sweet bluebell.

Whence came that rising in my throat,
    That dimness in my eyes?
Why did those burning drops distil,
    Those bitter feelings rise?

Oh, that lone flower recalled to me
    My happy childhood's hours,
When bluebells seemed like fairy gifts,
    A prize among the flowers.

Those sunny days of merriment
    When heart and soul were free,

And when I dwelt with kindred hearts
   That loved and cared for me.

I had not then mid heartless crowds
   To spend a thankless life,
In seeking after others' weal
   With anxious toil and strife.

'Sad wanderer, weep those blissful times
   That never may return!'
The lovely floweret seemed to say,
   · And thus it made me mourn.

Appeal

Oh, I am very weary,
   Though tears no longer flow;
My eyes are tired of weeping,
   My heart is sick of woe;

My life is very lonely,
   My days pass heavily,
I'm weary of repining;
   Wilt thou not come to me?

Oh, didst thou know my longings
    For thee, from day to day,
My hopes, so often blighted,
    Thou wouldst not thus delay!

Night

I love the silent hour of night,
    For blissful dreams may then arise,
Revealing to my charmed sight
    What may not bless my waking eyes.

And then a voice may meet my ear,
    That death has silenced long ago;
And hope and rapture may appear
    Instead of solitude and woe.

Cold in the grave for years has lain
    The form it was my bliss to see;
And only dreams can bring again
    The darling of my heart to me.

If This Be All

O God! if this indeed be all
   That Life can show to me;
If on my aching brow may fall
   No freshening dew from Thee;

If with no brighter light than this
   The lamp of hope may glow
And I may only *dream* of bliss,
   And wake to weary woe;

If friendship's solace must decay,
   When other joys are gone,
And love must keep so far away,
   While I go wandering on, –

Wandering and toiling without gain,
   The slave of others' will,
With constant care and frequent pain,
   Despised, forgotten still;

Grieving to look on vice and sin,
   Yet powerless to quell
The silent current from within,
   The outward torrent's swell;

While all the good I would impart,
    The feelings I would share,
Are driven backward to my heart,
    And turned to wormwood there;

If clouds must *ever* keep from sight
    The glories of the Sun,
And I must suffer Winter's blight,
    Ere Summer is begun:

If Life must be so full of care –
    Then call me soon to Thee;
Or give me strength enough to bear
    My load of misery.

The Narrow Way

Believe not those who say
    The upward path is smooth,
Lest thou shouldst stumble in the way,
    And faint before the truth.

It is the only road
    Unto the realms of joy;
But he who seeks that blest abode
    Must all his powers employ.

Bright hopes and pure delights
  Upon his course may beam,
And there, amid the sternest heights,
  The sweetest flowerets gleam.

On all her breezes borne,
  Earth yields no scents like those;
But he that dares not grasp the thorn
  Should never crave the rose.

Arm – arm thee for the fight!
  Cast useless loads away;
Watch through the darkest hours of night,
  Toil through the hottest day.

Crush pride into the dust,
  Or thou must needs be slack;
And trample down rebellious lust,
  Or it will hold thee back.

Seek not thy honour here;
  Waive pleasure and renown;
The world's dread scoff undaunted bear,
  And face its deadliest frown.

To labour and to love,
  To pardon and endure,
To lift thy heart to God above,
  And keep thy conscience pure;

Be this thy constant aim,
  Thy hope, thy chief delight;
What matter who should whisper blame,
  Or who should scorn or slight?

What matter, if thy God approve,
  And if, within thy breast,
Thou feel the comfort of His love,
  The earnest of His rest?

Last Lines

A dreadful darkness closes in
  On my bewildered mind;
O let me suffer and not sin,
  Be tortured yet resigned.

Through all this world of blinding mist
  Still let me look to thee,
And give me courage to resist
  The Tempter, till he flee.

Weary I am – O give me strength,
  And leave me not to faint:
Say thou wilt comfort me at length
  And pity my complaint.

I've begged to serve thee heart and soul,
  To sacrifice to Thee
No niggard portion, but the whole
  Of my identity.

I hoped amid the brave and strong
  My portioned task might lie,
To toil amid the labouring throng
  With purpose keen and high;

But thou hast fixed another part,
  And thou hast fixed it well;
I said so with my breaking heart
  When first the anguish fell.

O thou hast taken my delight
  And hope of life away,
And bid me watch the painful night
  And wait the weary day.

The hope and the delight were thine:
  I bless thee for their loan;
I gave thee while I deemed them mine
  Too little thanks, I own.

Shall I with joy thy blessings share
  And not endure their loss;

Or hope the martyr's crown to wear
    And cast away the cross?

These weary hours will not be lost,
    These days of passive misery,
These nights of darkness, anguish-tost,
    If I can fix my heart on thee.

The wretch that weak and weary lies
    Crushed with sorrow, worn with pain,
Still to Heaven may lift his eyes
    And strive and labour not in vain;

Weak and weary though I lie
    Crushed with sorrow, worn with pain,
I may lift to Heaven mine eye
    And strive and labour not in vain;

That inward strife against the sins
    That ever wait on suffering
To strike wherever first begins
    Each ill that would corruption bring;

That secret labour to sustain
    With humble patience every blow;
To gather fortitude from pain
    And hope and holiness from woe.

Thus let me serve thee from my heart
   Whate'er may be my written fate,
Whether thus early to depart
   Or yet a while to wait.

If thou shouldst bring me back to life,
   More humbled I should be,
More wise, more strengthened for the strife,
   More apt to lean on thee.

Should Death be standing at the gate,
   Thus should I keep my vow;
         But hard whate'er my future fate,
So let me serve thee now.